AF080567

The Words I Couldn't Say

I've written it all down,

For you to read.

I want to be seen, heard, understood.

Grey

BLUEROSE PUBLISHERS
India | U.K.

Copyright © Grey 2023

All rights reserved by author. No part of this publication may be reproduced, stored in a retrieval system or transmitted in any form or by any means, electronic, mechanical, photocopying, recording or otherwise, without the prior permission of the author. Although every precaution has been taken to verify the accuracy of the information contained herein, the publisher assume no responsibility for any errors or omissions. No liability is assumed for damages that may result from the use of information contained within.

BlueRose Publishers takes no responsibility for any damages, losses, or liabilities that may arise from the use or misuse of the information, products, or services provided in this publication.

For permissions requests or inquiries regarding this publication, please contact:

BLUEROSE PUBLISHERS
www.BlueRoseONE.com
info@bluerosepublishers.com
+91 8882 898 898
+4407342408967

ISBN: 978-93-5819-788-4

First Edition: September 2023

Index

Acknowledgement

The Words I Couldn't Say

Live Up

Spend My Time With You

Let Me

Imagine

Just The Things You Say

End

Cold

Gone

Ray

A Chair On The Way

Baggage

Shameful

Absence: Yours

Feelings: Mutual

Just Me

To You

Tired

Abyss

Majestic Falls

Love Again?

Pain, Would You Be My Friend?

Living For

Family

Accept And Going

Fire

Away

And So I Chose

Failure

Let Go

My Wish

Take Care Of Yourself Bubs

Acknowledgment

I wouldn't be where I am today without them. People who have helped me go on and found me when I was lost are the ones who brought me here. I have been lost for too long, alone, empty, and homeless. I didn't know where I belonged.

My friends, colleagues, family, and plenty of people I met for the first time helped in my time of need. I would go into detail about how I ran away umpteenth times and spent days in distant places, but that is another story to tell. I mean it from the deepest corner of my heart when I say I would be nothing without them.

I want to thank my parents and grandparents here, who shaped me into a decent person and gave me the values I consider important today. Although they never directly supported my career, they worried about my well-being, and small things added. In secondary school, my English teacher, Jayshankar Tiwari, has the credit for developing my interest in literature. I never enjoyed other classes as much as I did yours, sir!

However, these are not my last words of thanks and resentment, as this book is about it all.

Dedicated

To

You

You who see me, hear me out, understand me.

The Words I Couldn't Say

The words, saying them was saying too much,

The words that were never heard.

The words I couldn't say.

At a point in time, you stop saying everything you feel,

You start accepting things as they are.

You don't express much,

You keep it all inside.

The words I couldn't say, I've written it all down,

For you to read.

I want to be seen, heard, understood.

Has the art taken out a part of you?

Artist

I dreamt a dream,
Set out on a journey,
Away from everyone I could have known,
I didn't feel like it,
To know or meet them.

I chased that dream,
Always lost in it,
Never liked the life I could have loved,
Because I didn't like it,
It wasn't the life I wanted.

I lived in dreams, Or did I?

I wonder if I ever lived at all,

Some say to dream is to live

And the journey to the summit is it all.

But when you voyage through tides of life,

Sailing to reach the far-away goal,

You taste the salts and sand on the road.

The love for your dream keeps you going,

But the rollercoaster ride breaks you down,
And that's where you pick the pain
And you use it to paint your canvas.

You've made that masterpiece,
And yet, what have become of you,
You are far from everyone you could have loved,
And those you loved on the way abandoned you.

You've painted it out on the canvas,
But there's a hole inside of you,
When you caress your chest, why's it hollow?
Has the art taken out a part of you?

You might be grateful for the pain,
Because it makes you an artist,
But Grey, you know you are not happy,
But you wouldn't been happier even if,

Even if you never went after it.

Because that's who you are, and you can't settle for less,

This is the life you'll choose, Always,

If we let you choose over and over again.

But not the healing pain I got,

When I tried to look for someone special

Live Up

I sought someone to heal me,

who would hide me in her bosom and let me cry

I sought someone to feel me,

I thought I would blossom, and she'll be the reason why,

That someone would conceal me,

When I'm hit by words sharper than a knife

Just having her beside me would thrill me,

And together, we would share a happy life.

But not the healing pain I got,

When I tried to look for someone special

And Hope kept me busy, so I forgot
to take care of myself amidst all the hassle

I thought once I found her, it'll be all
so easy, we could be cozy and skip this bustle

But now I know life's just hard,
And don't look for someone was my lesson.

I've got me and some people in my life
It might not feel magical or complete, but yet,
Friends and family can keep me alive
And I can try to live up the life left.

I'll just spend my time with you.

Spend My Time With You

I will spend my time with you.

The words are too hard to utter,

and things are difficult to share.

I'll keep them inside my heart

and just spend my time with you.

I'll skip the hard part of telling you how I feel.

I can't put our friendship on the line.

I'll just spend my time with you.

So hold my hand and let me take you to our safe haven.

Let Me

How can I express that's it's alright to let me inside of your mind,

You don't have to go through second thoughts about us.

You don't have to check for no red flags,

Or take a rain check.

Babe, you don't have to worry if I'm good for you or if we're going to be good together,

Because I've thought about it all.

I've gone through such wondering already,

And all I want you to do is trust me.

So hold my hand and let me take you to our safe haven.

In the moments I'll look into your eyes,

And know that it's just me and you.

Imagine

Imagine a day flowing by,

I could write and write,

With nothing else to do,

Just to ink every corner that's white.

I would write to tell you,

About why I think the wind blows,

And why do the birds sing in,

Distant places one rarely knows.

I know I would have to tell you,

About the dreamy woods, I run off to,

And those grey roads I wearily trod,

When my eyes need a change of view.

It won't be for long but,

I would be lost, too,

In the moments I'll look into your eyes,

And know that it's just me and you.

Your words touch me, and words from my soul start to flow.

Just The Things You Say

Your words have an effect on me.

They make me pause, think, and wonder.

Your words touch me, and words from my soul start to flow.

Just the things you say and the perspective you present,

Seeing the world through your eyes steals me from all the noise and bustle of the world around me.

I discover the beauty in life that I forgot of,

And remember to appreciate the things around me that tend to drift away from me.

They drift away because I stop seeing because I get too blind, too busy in the hoo-ha of the material world.

But your words, oh, just the things you say!

You've pulled me closer to the truth again.

And I know I'll sink again,

But that doesn't stop me from admiring the fresh air as I float on the surface with you.

Moments end shortly, and memories span for years

End

Today won't last long,

The sun will soon set and cover everything in the dark.

A lovely moment with you wouldn't last long,

Tomorrow, we will just turn into bygones.

The short-lived time we will spend together,

Will only end up as memories,

We might separate, change, or cease to exist,

And in the end, I will be left alone.

In the end,

Every attachment will need to be rid of,

Everyone in life would ask to let go,

People who know me will drift apart,

Good things seldom last.

I'll, once again, be clad in darkness,

Empty and all alone,

Why did we meet, then?

Why did we stay together at all?

Moments end shortly, and memories span for years

I know I'll obsess over these memories,

I'll stay attached for long and think about you,

It is a sad fate that life has for us,

We spend much of it reminiscing over the things we did together,

And the things we said we would do,

but never got the chance to.

How can love turn into indifference suddenly?

Cold

She decided that we were over.

She wouldn't listen to me anymore,

She wouldn't hear a word I say.

No entreaty, no plea, no request to talk just once, would she accept.

She suddenly became so cold, like a stranger.

How can someone suddenly stop caring?

How can love turn into indifference suddenly?

I wasn't born with trust issues or fear of abandonment.

I guess the world was just not trustworthy.

But your love is gone, and now there's emptiness.

Gone

You liked me. You smiled at me.

You laughed with me. You loved me.

You lived with me.

You got hurt by me.

We fought. You hated me.

You disliked me.

You left me.

I didn't change.

I love you, but I am hurt too.

I made you smile, and I hurt you too.

I understand you,

And often, I didn't understand you.

And when I hurt you,

You didn't understand me.

I can clearly see

That you didn't understand me

And what I went through.

I was yours to love and take care of,

I wanted you to understand me, too.

But you chose to leave.

I hurt you, and you're scared of me now.

You're sick of me now.

And though how much I feel like it is unfair

And how much I'm sad that you didn't understand me,

I still want you.

I still hope things change for good. I hope you realize that these demons are in me,

The demon isn't me.

These issues aren't us or me,

They are in me.

I hope,

but I've little hope.

I've never seen you so cold before,

This side of you scares me.

I know I've lost you.

And lost a part of me with you.

This pain isn't anything,

What makes me sad is that I'm never gonna get your love again.

I hurt you, and you can hurt me too,

But your love is gone, and now there's just emptiness. You are gone.

We *will* never have these moments *again.*

Hey

We were together, and things we did,

Made me smile back then.

But it haunts me now.

The songs I used to sing hit hard,

And the memories play in slow motion in my head,

A never-ending film.

Everything is gone,

But the worst stayed.

You're gone.

You'll never laugh with me again,

We will never be in love with each other again.

We will never have these moments again.

How can I fill this emptiness?

How can I live without someone anymore?

A Chair On The Way

The forestland slid beneath my regular strides,
I covered it with my fearsome grace.
Though trees passed me on both sides,
None could interrupt my terrific pace.
I could have walked tirelessly for nights and days.

But some miles later, a chair was kept
Under a tree of the same wood brown.
I ignored it and continued to the woods' depth
But a little later, I stopped and gave me a frown.
I had enough time to rest for some time unknown.

I lowered me on the Chair—
Oh, how wonderful it was to rest!
And looked at others with a glare
Because I possessed the best.

A long later, I lifted it above my chest
And carried the same everywhere.

Amazed, I carried and sat on it
Till I was dazed after months, four,
When it fell off a cliff and broke split,
And I was angry for the loss and broke it more.
"How can I fill this emptiness?
How can I live without a chair any more?"

I cried so long that I cried out of
My mind the reason I cried for,
When I tried to recall— "What?
A chair is for what I cried so far!"
At once, I stood and left the place.
Years it took to regain the pace
And years it took to learn to refrain—

*And years later, I crossed a chair of the same wood
brown*

*This time, I rested, rejoiced, and left it there
without a frown.*

Would you run away again?

If I talked about how messed up I've been since you left?

Baggage

Would you run away again

If I talked about how messed up I've been since you left?

Would my feelings be a burden to you?

It's so sad that

I can't even cry about what

I've been going through since you left,

Because I don't know a lot of people

who will understand.

And I can't talk about it to you,

Because you'll probably start to wonder why we have a problem like this.

Your solution is always ending this conversation,

Ending us,

Because you don't really like to go through problems like this.

In this way, you'll shake yourself off the troubles I create.

But they won't be solved for me because I'll still feel the same.

I'll keep feeling the same unless I talk to you about it and get a warm reply.

Something that can calm the storm inside my mind.

Forgetting isn't always an answer.

But I can't talk to you about it,

Since I'm scared to lose you,

Forever.

And I'll always be ashamed of myself.

Shameful

I'm ashamed of myself,

Of the way I handled it,

Of the person I became to her,

I wish I could have been better.

I'm ashamed of the person she now knows me as.

When she asked me for space, I clung on,

She gave me signs that she's lost interest,

But I didn't read them,

And instead freaked out when she started changing.

I should have stopped when she dodged

the questions about the guy she's with now,

She said nothing was going on, and I should have believed her,

I shouldn't have figured out where she was lying,

Should have pretended to believe her.

I should have been okay with how things were changing,

I'm ashamed because when she asked me to get used to talking to her barely,

I should have been patient,

Instead, I got desperate,

She'll just remember me as a pathetic despo now,

And I'll always be ashamed of myself.

It couldn't be a lie,

Just the pain was proof enough that it was real.

Absence: Yours

It couldn't be a lie,

Just the pain was proof enough that it was real.

You're still in my sight,

Though you ran away in the wake of our first ordeal.

Can't blame you for it, though,

Can't say our happy moments mattered more than the pain I gave.

You were all I needed,

But I'm not sure if I showed you the love I have.

All the faults were mine, and I'm always so sincere about this,

And yet, honey, I don't know why you think I can ever get tired of you,

Feelings: Mutual

All the faults were mine, and I'm always so sincere about this,

And yet, honey, I don't know why you think I can ever get tired of you,

Ah, you think I don't know if you're good enough,

But there was never a doubt about it.

You're all I wanted, and I'd be blessed if I could deserve you.

I'd be so happy to have you, but I know I hurt you.

You're saying you'll try; that's giving me hope,

and I can't help thinking we can figure it out if we stick together.

But still, I can't stop worrying about you

because being with me for you means,

Going through all the pain that I bring,

And I don't know if you deserve that.

The you in my head was all me,

My creation, my imagination, all me,

Just Me

There was no you, it was me, and it'll be me always.
The you in my head was all me,

My creation, my imagination, all me,
It wasn't you, I was the one guilty,
Because I hurt myself over and again, infinite times,
I fell too fast, too hard, over and again,
It was me all along,
You never asked me to love you,
You never wanted me as I wanted you,
You never loved me, and I shouldn't have, too.

There was no you,
It was me all along,
I keep hurting myself.
And I can't stop it,
Because I have no control over it.

Yet I still feel drawn to you.

Though I am hurt too, from what happened,

I can't turn my back on you.

To You

The roads appear deserted,

The world around me got colder,

The flowers lost their meaning,

Everyone started to appear rude since you left.

Now, the cold mornings are not refreshing anymore,

Nor are the empty streets lovely.

Roaming around at 4 am in the morning is burdensome now.

Can't be bothered.

Yet I still feel drawn to you.

Though I am hurt too, from what happened,

I can't turn my back on you.

It felt lively and exciting

And now I feel like I'm just going on,

It's not okay anymore after you left.

But are things better for you?

Is life happier apart?

Expectations only hurt,

And I feel like closing myself inside my shell,

With little interactions and disappointment to my soul from the outer world.

Tired

Thinking hard, trying to get your attention,

Trying to make you feel at ease,

Trying to make you understand,

Trying to show you that we can,

Trying to impress you,

Trying to give you love,

Trying and trying and tired.

But I feel like I've tried enough.

But if persevering is right, and stopping is giving up,

And I should probably keep it up if I want to win your love,

But I feel like it's not a fair fight,

And my self-esteem can't seem to bear the hurt.

I haven't yet made up my mind,

But right now, I feel like letting go of you.

As long as I keep holding onto you, and unless you show me the light,

Unless you bother to take my hand and guide me,

Unless you feel the need to care about me and lead us,

Unless then, I will still be in this dark uncertainty.

I'm so uneasy around the darkness.

Right now, I feel like letting go,

I feel like forgetting everything,

Expectations only hurt,

And I feel like closing myself inside my shell,

With little interactions and disappointment to my soul from the outer world.

I'm tired of the hurt.

I've made up my mind,

I'm leaving it all to you.

I'm leaving it all behind, retreating on the road

That once led me to you.

Abyss

Letting go of expectations and attachments,

I'm accepting this lone journey as mine.

I've made up my mind,

I'm leaving it all to you.

I'm leaving it all behind, retreating on the road

That once led me to you.

Behind me, I leave all the regrets and desires, my wish, and you,

You had made up your mind, and now me too,

And I'm giving up trying to bring the change in you.

I'm letting it all be, not opposing nor enforcing,

And the doors of my home will be,

Forever welcoming,

And birds on your way will be merry,

Whispering,

If you ever decide to walk the road that leads to me,

If you meet the change that I tried to bring in you.

Changing to revert to who you became after you changed,

Changing back to the old loving self you've been.

Come find me when you love me again.

***Which, while I focussed on stains
over a beautiful painting,***

Had gone?

Majestic Falls

The spectacular woods deliberately tinged fresh green,

The majestic falls offered beats for birds' songs.

The kaleidoscopic streaks replaced the fear of the unseen

And the crimson, besides itself, could deepen only the dawn.

Oh! I'm not exhaling and inhaling in impressive ways.

Whoa! The sun is well above the horizon;

Did it display the marveling work of the first rays

Like they say, which, here, makes special the dawn?

Did I miss something for which I trod all the way alone,

Which, while I focussed on stains over a beautiful painting,

Had gone?

Beware! When you go before a looking glass.

" Oh! But why? What does it take to?"

Know— Can you afford a chance?

It can build but also break you.

Through her, a looking glass, I saw flaws

In my otherwise beautiful face.

Immaterial is the number of days that have passed

Since then, unblurred, still, is that image.

Like the continuous roaring wind that,

To its own accord, does the desert shape

Or the sailor, whose ear heard some solitary vows,

Which he himself hissed out after a sharp intake,

This spirit to be on the battlefield constantly has never withered–

For, when on some part of this voyage,

For matching my plod, down a looking glass slows,

Should never to her eyes, it show any blemish,

Should always the superbness of her object keep us close.

When there's nothing left inside us,

How can we love again?

Love Again?

Love,

But all we know is to hurt,

We are looking for love from someone else,

But loving is hard,

It's easier to hurt someone.

It is easier to inflict that pain on them

Than to put their happiness before us,

It's hard to be kind when you are hurt

It takes courage and sacrifice to love.

We want someone to love us,

But is there enough love left in them,

They have been hurt, too,

And we have hurt people over again.

The words that injure me,

I have said the same to someone else,

And we have done this to one another,

Until every one of us has felt it,

Over again.

We are hurt to our bones,

Our soul is scarred by betrayal and fake promises,

We all are too skeptical to trust,

And if we do trust, doubts flood our brains.

Our past will always haunt us,

Those memories will never let us love again.

Who will love us, then?

When every one of us is engulfed in pain.

Where will that love and romance come from?

When there's nothing left inside us,

How can we love again?

It hurts so much when you dream of good things

Pain, Would You Be My Friend?

Memories,

Of the short-lived moments I cherish,

I'm in pain, but I'll make it my friend,

It's not that I like pain any bit,

But accepting it gives my mind peace,

And I believe that getting used to it will make me strong.

It hurts so much more when you dream of good things,

When those expectations are hurt by someone you had faith in,

But if I befriend pain and let it stay right here by me,

I know it won't leave my side,

And although it's not a company I crave for,

I want to stop dreaming of someone's company anymore,

So, if a little bit of pain and loneliness is all it takes not to be disappointed,

I'd happily stay alone on my lone Island forever,

Because I don't want to hope for your company ever,

I don't want to get hurt again.

I've seen it all through,

Why, then, do I keep going on?

What am I living for?

Living For

I know how it goes and how it ends,

I've seen it all through,

Why, then, do I keep going on?

What am I living for?

I've been hurt by people,

Watched the sweetest ones change,

Someone who I thought was exceptionally lovely,

And could never do anything wrong,

Proved me wrong.

Why, then, do I keep going on?

I've seen the worst faces of people,

Their darkest selves, the cold hatred in their hearts,

The selfish, stone-cold indifference to the well-being of others,

And yet,

Why do I keep giving them another chance?

When everyone has let me down,

My family, or people whom I called friends,

Everyone,

Why, then, am I going on all alone?

When everyone taught me I shouldn't trust,

Why do, then, I keep giving in to hope,

What am I living for?

They arrived, stayed, and left,

But something has remained here.

Family

It lingers on,

Their presence,
The containers in the kitchen that have been moved,
The empty water bottles that lie in the corner of the room,
Draw my mind to things they did and said.

It was a short visit,
Ended before it began,
They arrived, stayed, and left,
But something has remained here.

Is it what it feels like to have a family?
When they were there, I didn't have to worry about things,
I could just leave it all to them,
They asked me if I ate and cooked for me,
Perhaps that's what it feels like to have a family.

It was quite short of a visit, actually, to think of much,

Of will I miss them,

I've grown so accustomed to living alone,

That it never crossed my mind,

This feeling right now is me missing them.

It is hard to live with memories of somewhere you're done,

Thus, here I am, starting a beginning again.

Accept And Keep Going

I reached with my eyes and froze

And froze my heart for a little longer.

The large patch; on three sides, the woods rose,

And no moonlight on darker corners yonder.

"Will I be able to do it again?"

I left it as I had left everything

else when something left me, which was crucial.

All my crucial uniqueness ceased to be,

The hobbies turned into burdens,

I shook them off to be set free.

Otherwise, my hands used to hang, my legs sprinting

Unafraid of the dark blankets, the forest loudly whispering

Joking continuously to drive off the ghosts (would be) pestering.

Now that is past, strength is gone

But the will, least the wish, has regrown.

It is hard to live with memories of somewhere you're done,

Thus, here I am, starting a beginning again.

I expected not the pace my legs have known.

I leaped; after a few steps, didn't stop

But slowed down—the signs all discouraging,

No moon around the horizon or the top,

With the dark night deadly gesturing,

With tracks on the sand of, perhaps, snakes

And shrill voices of the creatures sheltering.

Yet—I accepted, accelerated, and kept going.

And minutes later, revealed clouds, a moon,

A full, warm, yellow moon,

Smiling.

I don't want to destroy what's around me.

Fire

I know only I can contain,
The fire inside of me,
Calm me up and cool me down myself.

I don't want to let it out.
I don't want to destroy what's around me.

I'm far away from where my heart is.

Away

I want to steal away from here.

I want to go somewhere I can admire the beauty of mountains,

Of scarcely lit country roads,

Of a cliff view of a roaring seashore.

The picture is so vivid in my head

Like I can taste the experience of being there.

But I'm in the knowledge of the truth,

That I'm far away from where my heart is.

I chose hope over happiness.

And So I Chose

Choose, the voice in my head whispered.
Choose, the world said to me.

Choose between stability and hope.
Choose between happiness and comfort.
Choose, the voice insisted,
Choose before it's too late, Fear commanded.
Before you're left with no choice.

And so I chose,
I chose wisdom over impulse,
I chose comfort over passion,
I chose hope over happiness,
And I saved the latter for later.

Defeated and buried under the weight of broken dreams

It's like screaming for help from a far-off ocean,

Muffled.

Failure

I try to fit in their world.

And keep my world a secret

Inside the shell of my mind,

Filled with pieces of my broken dreams.

For a few hours every day,

I come back to the world I belong to.

*I'm not good at anything in their world or mine.
So I live a defeated life,*

Keeping a good distance from the people in their world,

Indulging only when necessary.

I gave away everything to be something in my world,

To become something that matters to me.

If I had to be powerless and weak and not have an identity in their world,

If I had to be absolutely invisible, ignored by everyone, and never looked upon.

Even if I had to live this way

It would be alright if I could be something in my world,

If I can get better at things that matter to me.

But I gave away everything I had in their world, rejected all the opportunities,

And came to the world I cared about

Only to realize I didn't stand a chance.

Lost in my world,

Defeated and buried under the weight of broken dreams,
Life like this,

Not just living as an invisible person,

It's like screaming for help from a far-off ocean,

Muffled,

Unheard.

I put my heart out there,

What else did I expect?

It was destined to be broken,

Every single time.

Let Go

Long I have wandered in the colorful world of romance,

Of love and hate, of broken promises and unfulfilled expectations,

Oh, how desperate I have been, looking for someone to love,

Hoping for someone to understand me and adore me dearly,

But I was never good enough.

Blinded by the dreams of sweet days and lovely life together,

I let them define and judge me,

Because I was greedy for their love,

And scared that if I did anything wrong,

They would leave me.

It is easy to see not all of it was love,

It was a mix of infatuation, obsession, my fear of abandonment, and loneliness,

I put my heart out there, always expecting and waiting for love,

I put my heart out there,

What else did I expect?

It was destined to be broken,

Every single time.

I am sick of people trying to use me,

People being selfish,

Changing to become someone else,

Showing their true colors,

Never keeping their promises,

And never seeing how much they hurt me.

I'm sick of it all,

I'll let go of any hope I had of finding someone understanding,

And keep my distance from people,

I don't want to be hurt again.

And we cross paths someday

And exist in pairs.

I wish.

My Wish

Sometimes in our lives, people come who make us feel complete and loved.

And ultimately, they leave,

Leaving us feeling alone, incomplete, and totally lost.

The world starts to appear as a vast space where you exist all alone and unknown.

Feels like this is the reality of life,

And love and romance we hear about,

It all seems to be a fairytale.

Something we believe in,

something our human mind craves for,

wishes so much that a thing like love might exist

so that we don't live this life all alone,

days after day,

just operating.

It might keep us going through hard stuff,

Our mind wishes for something like love to make living easier,

but does it exist?

Often, I start to believe a life-long romance is just fiction.

But I'm not gonna lie, how much I wish I am wrong.

Oh, how much I wish that my soulmate might really exist

And we cross paths someday,

And exist in pairs.

I wish.

Take Care Of Yourself Bubs

You will know the feeling of being adored by someone when all they see is you.

Take your time, but yeah,

Don't give yourself over to anyone until you are sure that they are really head over heels for you. Anything less only hurts you and has a tragic end. Love yourself, and don't give yourself over to just anyone.

However, I don't ask you to refrain from loving,

Love on, Live on.

PS: This one is for you. ;)

When it gets too hard,

Love yourself,

You're the only one you've got.

Love Yourself

Lost in sadness,

All you do is hurt.

You have a heart babe,

All you need to love.

When life pours on you,

Like the winter rain,

You can keep yourself warm.

When it gets too hard,

Love yourself,

You're the only one you've got.

So darling love yourself,

Oh you can love yourself

Baby love yourself,

You're the only one I got.

(From the lyrics of Love Yourself by Grey.

Yet to be released.)

I've said too much for a lifetime.

About The Author

Grey is a writer, poet, songwriter, singer, and music computer. His interest in arts and expression has always inclined him to write his heart out. He is beginning his career as an author and music artist.

His poetry and music speak of the lovely and tragic experiences of life, loneliness, falling in love, and separating. It's actually his real-life experience that is manifested in his works. He's said to write with a bittersweet mood, and the poems end with a lingering feeling.

The readers who relate to his words will also likely like his music. Here's hwo you can listen to Grey on all streaming platforms.
On:
https://linkfly.to/greyzx
Or
https://horizons.music.blog/links/

www.ingramcontent.com/pod-product-compliance
Lightning Source LLC
LaVergne TN
LVHW061619070526
838199LV00078B/7347